LLAMA STOPS TEASING

A book about MAKING FUN of others

Written by
Sue Graves

Illustrated by
Trevor Dunton

W
FRANKLIN WATTS
LONDON·SYDNEY

No one really liked Llama. He wasn't always very kind. He was always teasing everyone. One day, he whispered something about Hippo to Tiger.

Hippo was worried. He asked Llama what he was whispering about. Llama laughed and said he was **only teasing**. But Hippo felt sad.

Llama upset Little Lion, too. When Little Lion
couldn't reach the top bookshelf in the library,
Llama laughed and said he was **too small**.
He said lions should be big and strong.

Little Lion said Llama **was rude**.

Llama said he was only teasing.

On Wednesday, Monkey wore new shoes to school. They were bright green and had blue laces. Monkey was very pleased with them. Everyone said they were great but Llama teased him and said they looked **really silly**. Monkey was upset.

At playtime, Llama had a big bag of sweets.
He gave everyone a sweet except Elephant.

Tiger told Llama **not to be mean**.
But Llama said he was only teasing.

Soon it was time for After School Club.
Mr Croc took everyone down to the swamp.
He said they were going to make a den.
He said they had to **work together**.

13

Everyone worked hard. But suddenly Giraffe tripped over. He banged his head on a branch. Giraffe was upset and had a little cry.

Everyone rushed to make Giraffe feel better.
But Llama **just laughed**. He said Giraffe was
a baby for crying!

Everyone was cross with Llama. They said he was mean to laugh at others. They said they didn't want him to help them build the den.

Llama said he was **only teasing**.
Tiger told Llama that sometimes
teasing wasn't funny at all.

Llama felt sad. He didn't like everyone being cross with him. He went to see Mr Croc. He told Mr Croc he didn't mean to upset everyone. He thought his friends **would laugh** if he teased them.

Mr Croc said sometimes teasing could make others **unhappy**.

Mr Croc asked Llama how he would feel if someone teased him. Llama had a think. He thought about Little Lion and Monkey. He thought about Elephant and Giraffe, too. He told Mr Croc that he would be sad if someone teased him like that.

Mr Croc asked Llama what he could do to **put things right**. Llama said he should **say sorry**. He said he should think about how people would feel if he teased them.

20

Mr Croc said Llama should try and remember that everyone should be treated **with respect**. Llama said he would try very hard.

Llama went to see the others. He said **he was sorry** for teasing them. He said **he didn't mean to** make everyone unhappy. He gave everyone a **big hug**.

23

Everyone got back to work on the den. Llama **didn't tease** Giraffe when he fell into the swamp. He kindly **helped him** out.

He **didn't tease** Turtle when she flipped over on to her shell by mistake. He helped her flip back again.

Soon the den was ready. Everyone said it was the best den ever. Then Tiger built a campfire. But it wouldn't light. He **was worried** that Llama would tease him.

But Llama didn't. Instead he helped Tiger to light it. Everyone said Llama was very kind. Llama said it was much **nicer to be kind** than to tease others. Everyone agreed!

A note about sharing this book

The *Behaviour Matters* series has been developed to provide a starting point for further discussion on children's behaviour both in relation to themselves and others. The series is set in the jungle with animal characters reflecting typical behaviour traits often seen in young children.

Llama Stops Teasing

This story looks at why teasing is not always funny and can cause upset to others. It reminds children to treat others with the same respect and kindness that they would wish for themselves.

How to use the book

The book is designed for adults to share with either an individual child or a group of children, and as a starting point for discussion.

The book also provides visual support and repeated words and phrases to build reading confidence.

Before reading the story

Choose a time to read when you and the children are relaxed and have time to share the story.

Spend time looking at the illustrations and talk about what the book might be about before reading it together.

Encourage children to employ a phonics first approach to tackling new words by sounding the words out.

After reading, talk about the book with the children:

- Talk about the story with the children. Encourage them to retell the events in chronological order.

- Talk about teasing in general. Often teasing is gentle and can be funny. Ask the children to recall any such incidents from their own experiences. Explain that sometimes, as with Llama, teasing can cause unhappiness.

- Talk about the different ways Llama teases others. Why do the children think it would be hurtful to talk about someone behind their back? Why is it not kind to make someone feel foolish as Llama did with Elephant? Why was Monkey upset when Llama laughed at his new shoes?

- Ask the children to share their own experiences of teasing. Have they been teased by friends? Have they teased others? What happened?

- Spend time talking about why someone might tease others. In Llama's case he wanted to make his friends laugh. He thought they would like him if he was funny. What other reasons can the children think of?

- Discuss ways of dealing with unwanted teasing. Invite the children to suggest someone who could help them if teasing became unkind or disrespectful.

- Place the children into groups. Ask them to brainstorm how they might point out to someone that their teasing was causing unhappiness.

- At the end of the session, invite each group to share their findings with the others. Together, draw up a list of useful strategies to help deal with inappropriate teasing.

29

For Isabelle, William A, William G, George, Max, Emily,

Leo, Caspar, Felix, Tabitha, Phoebe and Harry –S.G.

Franklin Watts
First published in 2020 by
The Watts Publishing Group

Text © Franklin Watts 2020
Illustrations © Trevor Dunton 2020

The right of Trevor Dunton to be identified as the illustrator
of this Work has been asserted in accordance with the
Copyright, Designs and Patents Act, 1988.

Editor: Jackie Hamley
Designer: Cathryn Gilbert

A CIP catalogue record for this book is available
from the British Library.

ISBN 978 1 4451 7088 6 (paperback)

Printed in China

FSC
www.fsc.org
MIX
Paper from
responsible sources
FSC® C104740

Franklin Watts
An imprint of
Hachette Children's Group
Part of The Watts Publishing Group
Carmelite House
50 Victoria Embankment
London EC4Y 0DZ

Hachette Ireland
8 Castlecourt
Castleknock
Dublin 15
Ireland

Franklin Watts is a division of
Hachette Children's Books,
an Hachette UK company.
www.hachette.co.uk